l i k a

What shall I make?

STORY **Nandini Nayar**

ILLUSTRATIONS **Proiti Roy**

This one is for Ai and *her* Neeraj – NN

What Shall I Make? (English)
ISBN 978-81-8146-268-8
© *text* Nandini Nayar
© *illustrations* Proiti Roy
First published in India, 2006
Reprinted in 2008, 2009, 2011

design Radhika Menon

Published by
Tulika Publishers, 13 Prithvi Avenue First Street, Abhiramapuram, Chennai 600 018, India
email tulikabooks@vsnl.com *website* www.tulikabooks.com

Printed and bound by
Shree Balaji Pvt. Ltd, 82/2A Kamaraj Salai, Virugambakkam, Chennai 600 092, India

To order books visit www.tulikabooks.com

Neeraj's mother was kneading dough.

She was going to make chapatis.

She gave Neeraj some dough to play with.

Neeraj squeezed the dough.
"What shall I make?" he said.

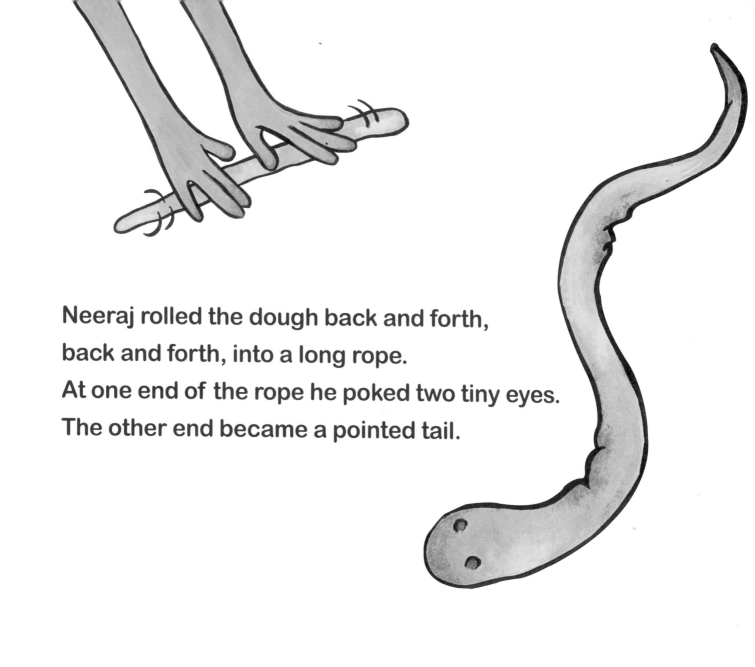

Neeraj rolled the dough back and forth,
back and forth, into a long rope.
At one end of the rope he poked two tiny eyes.
The other end became a pointed tail.

"A snake! A snake!"

"It's going to bite me!" Neeraj yelled.

"Roll it up, quick, quick!" his mother said. Neeraj quickly rolled up the snake. "What shall I make now?" Neeraj said.

Neeraj rolled the dough into a ball.

He patted it down, poked in two tiny eyes, and pulled out a nose.

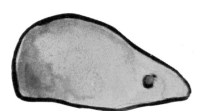

At the other end came a long tail.

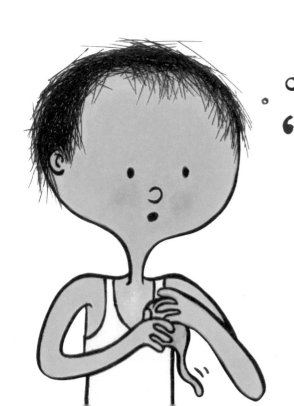

"A mouse! A mouse!"

Neeraj yelled. "It will run all over the house!"

"Roll it up, quick, quick!" his mother said. Neeraj quickly rolled up the mouse. "What shall I make now?" Neeraj said.

Neeraj rolled the dough into a ball.

He pinched off a small ball and stuck it on the big ball.

He made round eyes, and ears.

He gave it a tiny nose, and a tail.

"A cat! A cat!"

Neeraj yelled. "It's going to drink up all the milk!"

"Roll it up, quick, quick!" his mother said. "I can't!"
Neeraj said. "It's growing . . . and GROWING!"

"A lion! A lion!"

Neeraj yelled. "It's opening its mouth! And it's got big teeth!"

"Quick, quick!" his mother said. "You know what to do."

Neeraj grabbed the lion and rolled it up. Round and round. Round and round.

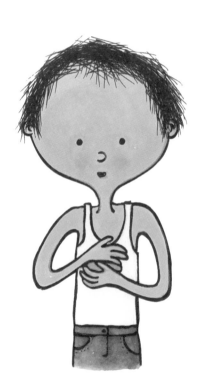

He rolled the dough into a ball. Round and smooth.

Then Neeraj pressed it flat. A small circle.

Neeraj rolled the circle bigger and bigger. A big round chapati.

His mother put it on the tava.

It puffed up.

Squeezed.

Pinched.

Patted.

Rolled flat and round.

Hot, light, puffy.

It was the best chapati Neeraj had ever eaten!